HEAR MY ROAR

A STORY OF FAMILY VIOLENCE

Gillian Watts

ART BY
Ben Hodson

annick press
toronto + new york + vancouver

Annick Press Ltd.

We acknowledge the support of the Canada Council for the Arts,
the Ontario Arts Council, and the Government of Canada through
the Book Publishing Industry Development Program (BPIDP) for
our publishing activities.

ONTARIO ARTS COUNCIL
CONSEIL DES ARTS DE L'ONTARIC

Cataloging in Publication
Watts, Gillian
    Hear my roar : a story of family violence / by Gillian Watts ;
art by Ben Hodson.

ISBN 978-1-55451-202-7 (bound).—ISBN 978-1-55451-201-0 (pbk.)

    1. Family violence—Comic books, strips, etc.—Juvenile fiction.
I. Hodson, Ben   II. Title.

PS8645.A8843H42 2009   j741.5'971   C2009-902576-0

Distributed in Canada by:
Firefly Books Ltd.
66 Leek Crescent
Richmond Hill, ON
L4B 1H1

Published in the U.S.A. by:
Annick Press (U.S.) Ltd.
Distributed in the U.S.A. by:
Firefly Books (U.S.) Inc.
P.O. Box 1338
Ellicott Station
Buffalo, NY 14205

Printed in China.

Visit us at: www.annickpress.com

The Bear family's story in *Hear My Roar* is only one example of how
domestic violence can unfold. The publisher wishes to stress that many
different scenarios and motivations can lead to violence in the home,
not all of which involve alcohol. For more information on how to deal
with an abuser and how to get help if you find yourself, or someone
you care about, in an abusive environment, please see the Afterword
and Resources sections at the end of this book.

For Robert and Alex, my two kids.
                    —G.W.

For my daughter Zoe.
With special thanks to my wife, May, and my mom, Gayle.
And to Jo Rioux, who is an amazing artist and teacher.
                    —B.H.

Foreword

Many people are affected by violence in the home. This book is intended to help children who have been exposed to family violence by giving them a framework for discussing their feelings, as well as a means of better understanding how their family's situation could be improved.

Hear My Roar is the story of a family in which the father becomes abusive to his wife and child. The mother becomes concerned when she realizes what effect the violence is having on her family. She turns to her family doctor for help and takes action to end the abuse. The story ends with Mama Bear and her son, Orsa, in a shelter. Papa Bear faces responsibility for his actions and is encouraged to seek help in resolving his problem behavior.

Children learn by watching how their families and friends behave. If they see violence being used to solve conflicts they may try using it as well, much the way Orsa begins to imitate his father. Violent behavior in the home leads to anxiety, fear, and even physical injury. It can also have enduring emotional and behavioral consequences for those affected. Children need to learn that violence is never an appropriate way to resolve conflict or to control others, that it does not have to be tolerated, and that action can be taken to stop it.

It is important to understand that the person committing the violence is solely responsible for his or her behavior. Victims of family violence must come to realize that they are not to blame and that there are ways to protect themselves and get help when they need it. Above all, children must learn that there are people who care about them and who will try to help them, whether they are relatives, friends, teachers, social workers, or other concerned members of the community. If you know or suspect that a child is suffering from family violence, it is important to contact someone who can help. Whether it's a doctor, a guidance counselor, or a social service agency, make it someone whom you trust to take effective action.

Note to Parents and Caregivers

The original version of this book was written to be read by a parent or caregiver. The publisher hopes that this new "graphic narrative" version will speak directly to young readers and encourage them to talk with someone in a position to help.

If you plan to read or give this book to a child who may need help, first read it yourself, noting any parallel situations that might be useful to discuss. Choose a quiet time and place to be with the child, and take as much time as you both need. Beginning readers may need help with some of the concepts, which could provide an opportunity to discuss any issues unique to the situation. You may decide to give more advanced readers time to check out the book on their own, and encourage them to share their thoughts and feelings afterward. This is a time to help children share what has been going on, understand that something can be done about it, and anticipate how the future might be made better for the whole family.

—Dr. Ty Hochban, *author of the first edition*

Summer

This is the Bear family: Mama, Papa, and little Orsa.

They live in the woods in a small wooden house. In the summer the woods are full of sweet berries, nuts, and seeds. Their garden has lots of tasty vegetables.

They like to picnic in the warm summer sun.

Time out for lessons. Mama is teaching Orsa his numbers, and how to read and write.

The Bear family is very busy in the summer.

These weeds make me so angry—they just keep coming back!

And why did you plant flowers? We can't eat flowers!

As summer passes ...

BANG BANG

BANG

Orsa, can't you do anything right?

Fall

In the fall, the weather gets colder and the trees lose their leaves. The wind grows stronger and the days get shorter. Food is harder to find. This year, fall comes early.

The Bears are working hard to prepare for winter.

13

The Bears are very tired from working so hard. Mama and Papa argue a lot. They're worried they won't be ready in time for winter.

You should have been ready for this bad weather. What do you do all day, anyway?

I do my best. I cook and clean and teach Orsa his lessons every day. And I have outside chores to do as well.

Don't talk back to me!

I spend all day in the forest trying to find us food and firewood. When I get home I'm cold and tired.

Give me some more wine!

Some bears drink homemade jack-berry wine to make them feel warm and to fill their empty bellies. Papa likes jack-berry wine, but it makes him act silly and angry.

C'mon, Orsa, smarten up! Don't act so stupid!

Don't you think you've had enough wine? You're going to have a sore head in the morning.

I don't care—I'll do what I want!

14

I'm sorry I've been so angry lately. I promise things will be better in the spring.

I forgive you. I think all we need is a good winter's sleep. I love you, dear.

And I love you too.

Spring

When the bears wake up, it's spring. But the weather is cold and wet. Mama and Papa have to find food to eat. They need dry wood to keep them warm. The house must be cleaned after the long winter.

Papa will feel better when he sees our tidy house and we have food to eat. All we need is a good spring. Then everything will be fine.

Grrr, there's no food, no wood!

Grr, this cold wind and rain!

Come and rest and have some food. Then you'll feel better.

I'm sick of dried berries! I'd rather go hungry than eat these old things.

CRASH

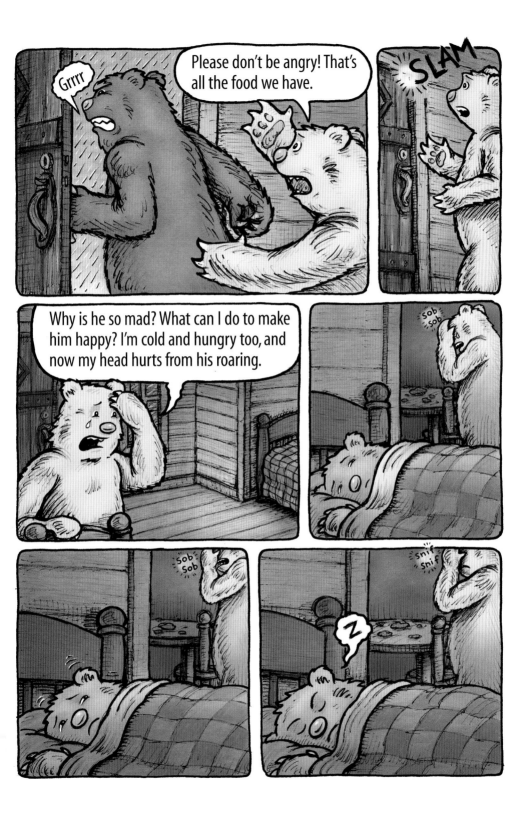

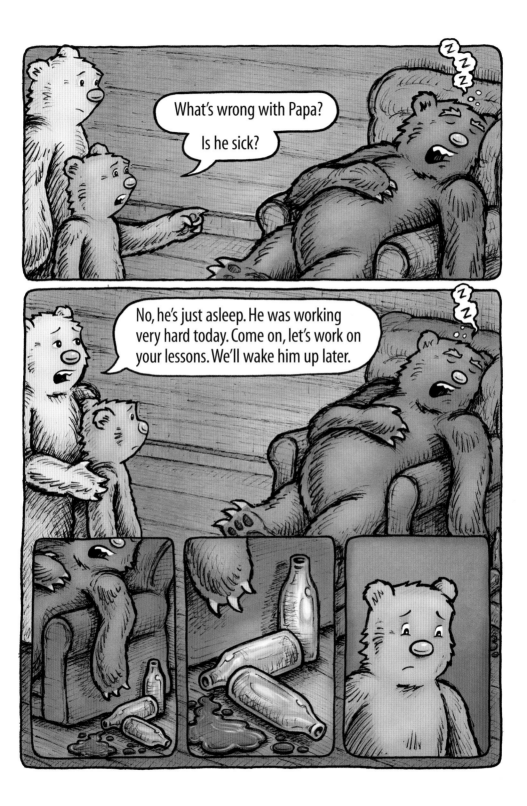

Things Get Worse

The days become warmer. Now there is more food. Spring is really here.

Orsa is playing with his toys.

A Visit to the Doctor

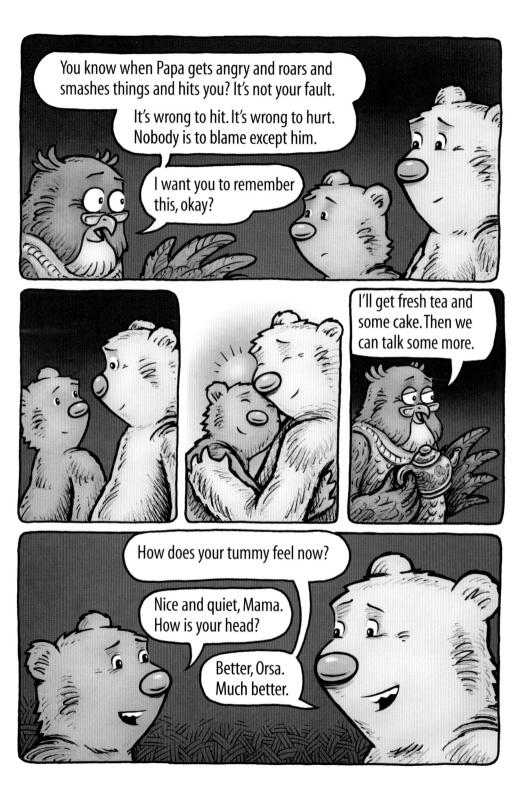

The three talk together for the rest of the afternoon.

The Last Straw

The next morning, while Papa is out.

Good morning, sleepy. Are you hungry?

I'm starving, Mama.

Where were you two yesterday?

Looking for shells at the beach, but we didn't find any. Please sit down and eat your breakfast.

No thanks. No time to eat. Orsa, hurry up and help me get some wood. We are going to make jackberry wine today.

Yes, Papa.

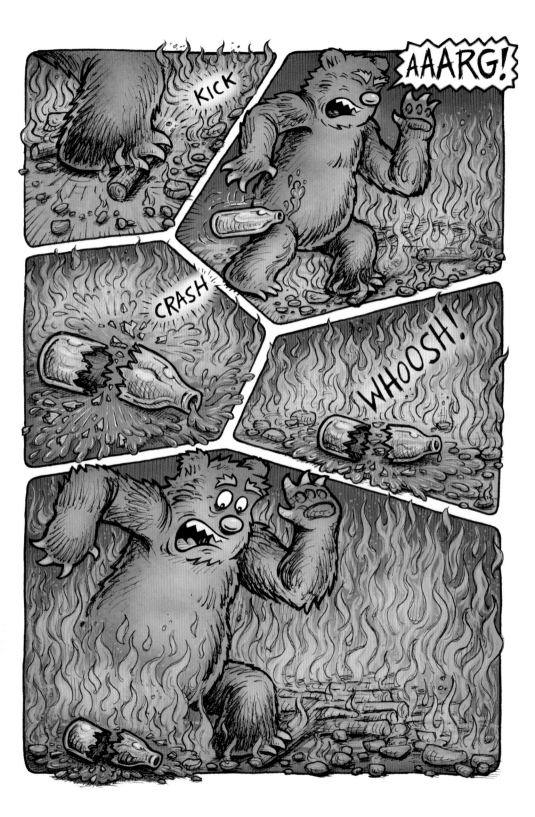

47

Doctor Owl's house.

Mama Bear tells Doctor Owl everything that happened.

I'm sorry to hear about this. I think you're right—you can't go back home now. I have friends at a shelter who can help you. They'll make sure you're safe.

I'll go and see Papa Bear to make sure he's all right. He is going to need help to stop his drinking and roaring.

On the path to the shelter.

Orsa, your father loves you very much. But he has a problem with his temper. He needs help and lots of time to stop all this hurting. Do you understand?

I think so.

Thanks for all of your help.

SHELTER
All welcome

Mama and Orsa arrive at the shelter and are taken in.

Papa's Remorse

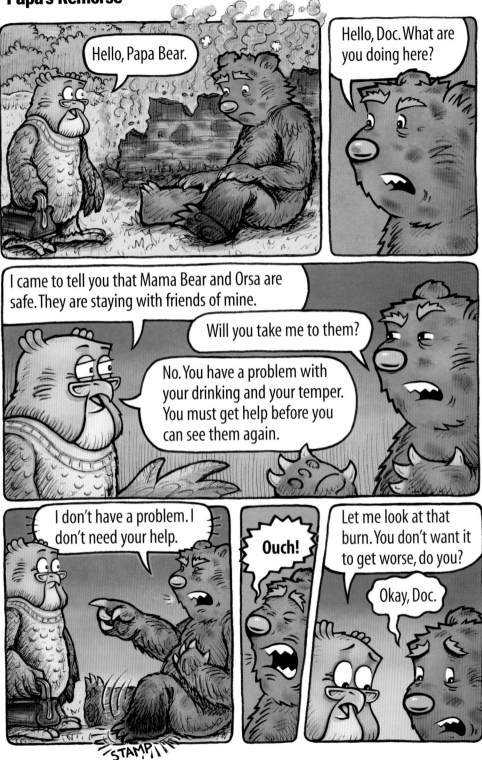

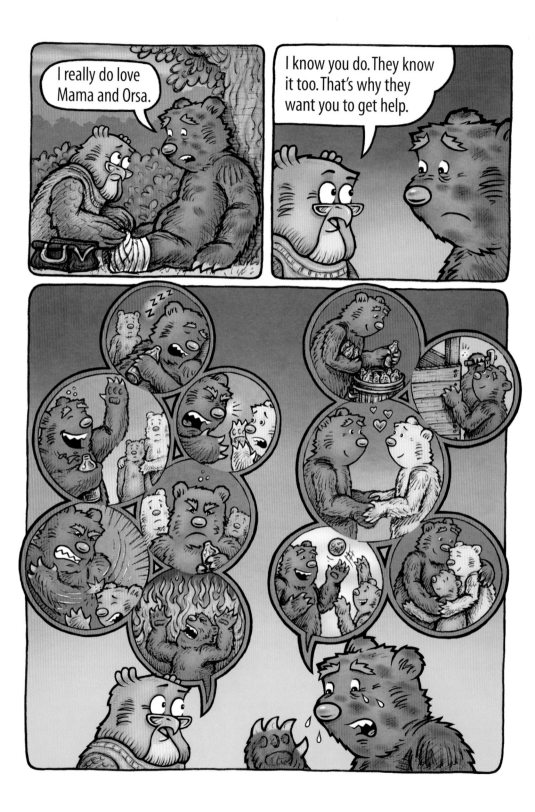

The End

Afterword

Recent research with young women and men shows that a significant number of them believe the use of violence in a dating or intimate relationship can be justified. This is a disturbing finding, and indicates that we need to be providing children and youth with much more education and information about what a healthy relationship is. If we are committed to reducing the incidents of domestic violence in our families and communities, we must expand our efforts to reach young people with critical information before they begin to date.

This book is one way we can begin dialogue with our children to help them understand that they have a right to live free from violence in their own homes. While the story in this book focuses some on the use of alcohol by the father, it is important to understand that alcohol does not cause violence. The book also highlights how the community must be involved in the solution to assist families to live safely and violence-free. In this story, it is the doctor who helps, but it could also be a law enforcement officer, attorney, faith leader, neighbor, friend, or family member. We all have a role in making our communities safer; for more information on how you can get involved, visit www.ncadv.org.

Rita Smith
Executive Director
National Coalition Against Domestic Violence
Denver, Colorado

For more information about family violence and how you can protect yourself and get help, please see the Resources section on page 55.

Resources

Free Hotlines

The following hotlines are open 24 hours a day, seven days a week, so you can call anytime. It's free to call, and whatever you discuss will be kept confidential. However, if you are in danger and need immediate help, call 9-1-1 instead.

In the U.S. you can call:
National Domestic Violence Hotline 1-800-799-7233
Childhelp USA (Child Abuse Hotline) 1-800-422-4453

In Canada you can call:
Kids Help Phone (for kids and teens) 1-800-668-6868
Parents Help Line 1-800-603-9100

Websites

The following websites offer information about domestic violence and resources to help those living with a violent parent or partner. Many of them also include lists of suggested reading for parents, children, and teenagers.

Ackerman Institute for the Family: www.ackerman.org

National Coalition Against Domestic Violence: www.ncadv.org

National Child Traumatic Stress Network: www.nctsnet.org

Child Witness to Violence Project: www.childwitnesstoviolence.org

StopFamilyViolence.org: www.stopfamilyviolence.org

Family Violence Prevention Fund: endabuse.org

Childhelp: Prevention and Treatment of Child Abuse: www.childhelp.org

Prevent Child Abuse America: www.preventchildabuse.org/index.shtml

Books for Parents

The Batterer as Parent: Addressing the Impact of Domestic Violence on Family Dynamics by L. Bancroft and J. Silverman. Thousand Oaks, CA: Sage Publications, 2002.

Children Who See Too Much by Betsy McAlister Groves. Boston: Beacon Press, 2003.

Hope and Healing: A Caregiver's Guide to Helping Young Children Affected by Trauma by Kathleen Fitzgerald Rice and Betsy McAlister Groves. Washington: Zero to Three, 2005.

The Impact of Family Violence on Children and Adolescents by Javad H. Kashani and Wesley D. Allan. Thousand Oaks, CA: Sage Publications, 1998.

When Dad Hurts Mom: Helping Your Children Heal the Wounds of Witnessing Abuse by L. Bancroft. New York: G.P. Putnam's Sons, 2004.

When Violence Begins at Home: A Comprehensive Guide to Understanding and Ending Domestic Abuse by K.J. Wilson. Alameda, CA: Hunter House, 1997.

Books for Children and Teenagers

Clover's Secret: Helping Kids Cope with Domestic Violence by Christine M. Winn and David Walsh. Minneapolis, MN: Fairview Press, 1996.

A Family That Fights by Sharon Chesler Bernstein and Karen Ritz. Morton Grove, IL: Albert Whitman & Company, 1991.

Mommy and Daddy Are Fighting by Susan Paris. Seattle, WA: Seal Press, 1985.

Something Is Wrong at My House: A Book about Parent's Fighting by Diane Davis. Seattle, WA: Parenting Press, 1984.

The Words Hurt: Helping Children Cope with Verbal Abuse by Chris Loftis and Catharine Gallagher. Far Hills, NJ: New Horizon Press, 1997.